DEATH BY EXPOSURE

ALSO BY ERIC WALTERS

DEATH
BY EXPOSURE

An Interactive Mystery

ERIC WALTERS
and KEVIN SPREEKMEESTER

An imprint of
Beach Holme Publishing
Vancouver

This book is published by Beach Holme Publishing, Suite 1010, 409 Granville Street, Vancouver, B.C. V6C 1T2. *www.beachholme.bc.ca*. This is a Sandcastle Book.

The publisher gratefully acknowledges the financial support of the Canada Council for the Arts and of the British Columbia Arts Council. The publisher also acknowledges the financial assistance received from the Government of Canada through the Book Publishing Industry Development Program (BPIDP) for its publishing activities.

Editor: Michael Carroll
Production and Design: Jen Hamilton
Front Cover Photograph: Kevin Spreekmeester
Author Photograph (Eric Walters): Paula Esplen

Printed and bound in Canada by AGMV Marquis Imprimeur

National Library of Canada Cataloguing in Publication Data

Walters, Eric, 1957-
        Death by exposure : an interactive mystery / Eric Walters ; photographer, Kevin Spreekmeester.

"A Sandcastle Book."
ISBN 0-88878-442-2

        I. Spreekmeester, Kevin, 1960- II. Title.

PS8595.A598D41 2004   jC813'.54   C2003-910073-1

Visit Eric Walters at *www.interlog.com/~ewalters* and Kevin Spreekmeester at *www.bluedoorphoto.com.*

The authors especially thank Tourism Saskatchewan and the Nova Scotia Department of Tourism and Culture for their help with the contents of this book.

To this beautiful country
of Canada and the undiscovered treasures within.
−Eric Walters

To my wife, Sue, my son, Ben, and my daughter, Katie.
You continually support my dream of travelling to wonderful,
faraway places with my camera and pen, and love me so
much that the moment I leave I can't wait to be with
you again. What a fantastic life I have!
−Kevin Spreekmeester

CONTENTS

NOTE FROM THE AUTHORS

Death by Exposure is a unique hybrid book that fits within no set box. It combines mystery fiction with photography, geography, mapping, history, secret codes, and Internet exploration. In short, there's a lot to do in this book. At the heart of the story is the puzzle of who the man in the glacier is and how he came to be there. The key to the riddle might be found in the latitude and longitude of photographs the iceman appears to have taken. So, after reading the story and studying the photographs, you're encouraged to do a little geography sleuthing and mapping in "Fun with Latitude and Longitude." There may be a different number code that supplies the answers to the enigma of the iceman, and you're invited to take a look at "Fun with Secret Codes" to see if you can crack the cipher.

But there's more! At the end of the book you'll find notes on the photographs and some great Web sites you can visit to learn more about various places and things in Canada. And, if you have a creative knack, take a look again at the photographs and the fragments of writing, get some paper, and see if you can finish the iceman's story about each picture. The important things, though, are to explore, experiment, create, and enjoy!

DEATH BY EXPOSURE

"**I**'m not a helpless little kid, Mom!" Ben complained.

"I know you're not, but you *are* only twelve and your sister is only nine."

"It's not like I haven't baby-sat her before."

"I'm not a baby!" Julia exclaimed.

"Sometimes you act like it," Ben snapped.

"Look who's talking about being a–"

"Both of you stop it!" their mother said. "I know you've taken care of your sister before, but I've never left you two alone for the whole day."

"We'll be fine."

"Do you two really think you can get along together for the entire day?"

"No problem. We get along fine," Ben said.

"Since when?" their mother asked.

"Since always."

"Yeah," Julia agreed. "We only fight when you're around."

"If that's the case, maybe I should go away more often."

"I don't know about that," Ben said, "but you should go out today. We hardly have anything to eat."

"What do you mean?" their mother said. "There's plenty of food."

"Yeah, but there's nothing *good* to eat."

Their mother opened the refrigerator. "Nothing good? We have plenty of cheese and meat, and the fruit bowl is full and–"

Ben frowned. "I don't mean good for you. I mean *good*. There are no more cookies, and the only cereal we have left doesn't even have sugar in it, and Julia ate the last two fruit roll-ups–"

"That's because you ate the first four in the box!" Julia protested. "So those two belonged to me!"

"Well, I didn't eat half the cookies and–" Ben stopped in mid-sentence when he realized that was exactly what their mother was worried about. "And I guess I should have eaten only three of the fruit roll-ups. How about if Julia gets four out of the box you buy today?"

"That would be fair," Julia agreed.

Ben turned to his mother. "You better leave now if you want to get there and back before dark. You know Dad doesn't like you driving these roads by yourself at night."

Their mother nodded. "At least I don't have to worry about the road conditions. These roads can be pretty dangerous in bad weather. But not today. They're clear and dry. I don't think there's ever been a winter with so little snow before."

"Nineteen twenty-seven," Julia said.

"What about 1927?" Ben asked.

"My teacher told our class that was the only year that had less snow than this year."

"And probably the only year that had less snow days when they cancelled the buses and we didn't have to go to school," Ben added.

Their mother smiled. "That's right. You haven't had one day this year when school had to be cancelled because of the weather."

"I know," Ben said. "It isn't fair. Last year we had seven snow days. Seven days to get together with my friends."

"Come on, Ben, it isn't like you don't see your friends when you go to school," their mother said.

"I see them, but it's a lot different to see them sitting at the next desk than to play pickup hockey on the pond, or build a snow fort, or have a snowball fight, or go tobogganing."

"I guess you're right there," their mother said. "I think this was also probably the worst winter we could have gotten you a toboggan for your birthday."

"You can say that again."

All Ben had had the chance to do since his birthday on January 14 was look at the biggest and best present he'd ever received—a new, shiny, hardwood toboggan. No snow had fallen for almost three weeks, and the little bit they'd seen before that had been melted by the last Chinook that had blown in from the Rockies.

"Don't worry, Ben, you'll be able to use it next year," Julia assured him.

"I'm not waiting for next year. I'm going to use it *this* year."

"Well, let's hope for some snow," their mother said. "Just not too much and not today."

"Then you *are* going shopping today?" Ben asked.

"Yes, I think I will." Ben's mother studied her son warily. "You seem awfully anxious to get me out of the house."

"I'm just anxious to get some *real* food into the house—that's all!"

Their mother cocked an eyebrow and gazed at Ben intently. Her son had a habit of glancing at the floor when he was lying or had a scheme up his sleeve. But this time he was looking her straight in the eye. Ben had realized recently that his mother knew he was up to something when he stared at the floor. He wasn't going to make that mistake anymore.

"Okay, then, tell you what," their mother finally said. "I'll just make sure the Thompsons are going to be home so you have somebody to call if there are any problems."

"Mom, Mr. and Mrs. Thompson must be ninety-nine years old!" Ben objected. "What problem do you think could come up that they could help me with?"

"I just like to know there's somebody you can call on if you need help."

"Fine," Ben said which, of course, meant it wasn't fine but there was no point in arguing.

❄ ❄ ❄

Ben and Julia stood at the big front window of their house and waved as their mother honked the horn of their red four-wheel-drive and drove off. They watched the vehicle hurry along the unpaved road, dip down, then reappear, only to cross the bridge over the river and vanish. There wasn't another living soul in sight. No people, no houses, no cars, no stores or malls or apartment buildings, just the green of the trees, the brilliant blue sky, and the mountains.

Ben remembered when they first moved here how he'd open the curtains each day and think, *Wow*, as he looked out the window at the mountains. This was certainly different than Calgary. But now it was no different than the day before or the day before that. Now they were just mountains. The only difference this year was that the mountains were brown and bare except for a rim of snowy white at the very top. He'd never seen them this brown in the three years his family had lived here.

Sometimes he still missed Calgary and all the friends he'd left behind. True, he liked the country, but he still wished for some of the things the city had to offer—movies, malls, video arcades, a place to roller-blade, and friends who lived just down the street. And when the friends he did have here weren't able to come out and play—like today because they were away for the weekend—that didn't leave him much to do or anybody to hang around with. That was the only reason he'd offered to baby-sit his little sister. Maybe there wasn't much to do, but at least he'd get paid for not doing anything. Besides, he did have an idea what they could do. He just had to set his plan in motion.

"You know," he said to Julia, "I was going to let you come with me on my toboggan the very first time I went down a hill. That is...if you wouldn't get scared."

"I wouldn't be scared," she insisted, and he knew she wasn't lying. Julia wasn't afraid of much. His mother said that growing up with a big brother made little sisters tough.

"Are you sure you wouldn't be afraid?" Ben asked as he went over and touched his toboggan. "This won't be so much a trip on a sled as it will be a ride on a rocket."

"I won't be afraid."

"So you'd be willing to ride on it?" he asked.

"Any time, any day!"

"How about anywhere?"

She gave him a quizzical glance.

"We could go tobogganing...today."

"Today? There's no snow."

"There's no snow *here*, but there is snow not far from here."

Instantly Julia knew what her brother was talking about, and a shiver went up her spine, one that had nothing to do with thinking about being cold.

"We could go to the glacier," Ben suggested.

"We're not supposed to go there. It's dangerous. Everybody knows that."

"How can a pile of snow and ice be dangerous?"

"Mom said people have died there."

Ben frowned. "Two people, ten years ago, and that was because they were trying to climb the steep side with picks and ropes. I'm just talking about walking a little way up the slope and sliding down. How can that hurt anybody?"

"Mom and Dad will kill you if they find out you went up there."

"And just how will they find out? I'm not going to tell them, so unless you do, nobody's ever going to know." Ben paused. "But if you're too much of a baby to go, I'll understand."

"I'm not a baby!" Julia protested, then smiled. She knew what her brother was doing, but she didn't care. She wanted to go, too.

The glacier was only a thirty-minute walk from their house. Today it seemed longer. Partly it was because of the toboggan. Since there was no snow, Ben had to carry it. As well, they were bundled up in their gloves, hats, boots, and snow pants, which made them very hot.

"There it is," Ben said, gesturing ahead.

Through the trees they could see the white of the glacier. That first glimpse gave Ben a surge of renewed energy. It had been a long walk, but it was going to pay off. They continued along the little path, plunging through more forest until they came out where the trees ended and the glacier loomed ahead. In front of them stood a field strewn with rocks, boulders, gravel, and mud.

"Wow, it's big," Julia said under her breath.

"It's a glacier. What did you expect?"

"I wasn't talking about the glacier," Julia said. "I meant the field–all the rocks and things."

"That was always there. Don't you remember it from when Dad brought us here two winters ago?"

"I remember Dad bringing us and we stood right about here at the edge of the forest," Julia said. "I just didn't think the glacier was that far from the forest."

Ben gazed out across the muddy, gravel-filled field that stretched before them. It did seem bigger. "I think you're right, but that would only make sense. Between last summer being such a scorcher and there being so little snow this year, I bet that a lot of the glacier melted away. Come on, let's get going." Ben started walking but turned around when he realized Julia hadn't moved. "Are you coming? Or are you waiting for it to come to you?"

Julia scowled, huffed, and then followed, catching up to Ben in a few seconds.

The field was made up of material that had been carried or crushed by the glacier, and then had been deposited by the retreating ice or the melting water. Dotting the landscape was a sprinkling of boulders, some as large as cars, a few as big as houses. As Ben and Julia approached the glacier, specific features became more visible. Here and there it resembled a high, steep wall. Elsewhere it seemed to slope gently. Across the whole front of the glacier there were spots where little fingers of ice–frozen runoff water–extended into the gravel field. These fingers in turn reached out from deep fractures, crevasses into the glacier.

"I think we should go down there," Ben said, pointing off to the side. "There's a slope and then there's ice that comes out across the gravel. Do you see anywhere better?"

Julia had been scanning the glacier and had noted the same place. "What time is it?" she asked.

"We have plenty of time."

"That's not what I asked."

Ben peered at his watch. "It's only ten-thirty. We'd be back in time even if we tobogganed for hours."

"But we're not doing it for hours. Just a few runs...right?"

"Just a few."

They kept on walking until the gravel under their feet changed to snow and then ice. Ben put down the toboggan and started to drag it behind him. The air had suddenly gotten colder. Julia tugged up the zipper on her parka and extracted her toque from one of the pockets. Placing the hat on her head, she pulled it down so that it covered her ears. Then she stamped her feet, grateful for her mukluks, even though she'd felt stupid wearing them earlier.

The slope began to rise more rapidly, and both of them felt the strain in their legs, the effort in their lungs. A couple of times Julia's feet slipped out from under her and she almost tumbled over. "How about we go from here?" she finally asked.

"Here? This low? We didn't come all this way to go down the bunny hill."

Ben continued to pull the toboggan up the slope. Reluctantly Julia trailed behind, keeping one eye on her brother and the other on the crevasse that dissected the slope into two long slices.

"How about here?" she asked again.

Ben sighed. "We'll go down the slope from here...the first time."

"And the next time?" Julia asked.

"We'll go a little bit higher next time, and a little bit higher after that. Unless you'd like to start from a lot higher now?"

She shook her head. "This is a good place to start."

Ben turned the toboggan around and sat on it, his legs off to the sides, digging into the snow to keep the toboggan from sliding. "Get on," he said to his sister.

Julia got on the back, pulled her legs up, and wrapped them around her brother.

"Here we go!" Ben announced. He raised his legs and pushed off with his hands. The toboggan began to move slowly at first, then picked up a little speed, and then more and more until it was flying. The wind rushed by, and the white of the snow was just a blur. The slope soon flattened out, and they continued to skitter along until finally coming to a stop.

"That was a ride!" Ben whooped as he jumped off the toboggan. "What did you think, Julia?"

She wanted to tell him how great it was, but shrugged instead. "It was okay."

"Okay?" Ben protested. "How can you say it was just okay?"

"From where I sat all I could see was your back. Maybe I should ride up front."

"You want to be in front and have me ride behind you?" Ben asked in amazement.

"At least *you* could see over my head. That's only fair."

Ben started to argue, but then asked, "How about a deal?"

"What sort of deal?"

"You can ride in front the next two times if you go on the back the five times after that."

"But we were only going down a few times, not eight!" she almost wailed.

Ben smiled. "Eight is a few. Besides, if you want to be in front, you should agree."

Julia smiled back. "Sure." What Ben didn't know was that she was smiling because she was going to ride down two times in front and then he was on his own.

They headed back up the slope, following the track left by the toboggan on the trip down. Finally they reached the place where they'd started the first run.

"This is good," Ben said.

"Here?" Julia questioned. She wanted this ride, with her in the front, to be a good, long one. "I think we should go higher...unless you're feeling scared."

Ben scoffed loudly. "You want higher, you'll get higher."

They continued upward for a while, then Ben stopped and turned the toboggan around, holding it in place while Julia got on. Instead of sitting, he put his hands on the toboggan and began to run, pushing it as hard as he could. He ran and ran and then jumped onto the back with a jolt.

The toboggan raced forward alarmingly, and Ben and Julia screeched in delight. They moved faster and faster as they descended, then Julia realized they weren't just going down the hill, but across its face toward the crevasse! She stuck out her feet and tried to dig them in to slow the toboggan down, but the snow and ice were too hard and there was no effect. Then, as they got closer and closer to the crevasse, Ben grabbed his sister and rolled off the toboggan with her. The two skidded and tumbled, head over heels, snow shooting into their faces and down their jackets until they skidded to a stop.

"Are you okay?" Ben asked, shaken.

Julia stood and shook one of her legs, which was sore. "I'm okay."

"Good. Let's get the toboggan and go home."

That was the first thing he'd said today—in a long time actually—that she agreed with. She looked around but couldn't see the toboggan anywhere. "Where *is* the toboggan?"

Ben pointed. "Down there."

"Down where?"

"In the crevasse. We have to go down and get it."

❄ ❄ ❄

Julia snorted. "This is the stupidest thing you've ever done."

"If it's so stupid, why are you here?" Ben asked as they worked their way along the frozen stream that led into the crevasse.

"Probably because I'm stupid, too. I must be if I'm following you."

"Well, you wouldn't have to follow me if you knew how to steer a toboggan!" Ben snapped.

"I know how to steer! It went crazy because somebody jumped onto the back and swerved it in a different direction!"

"If you knew how to steer, that wouldn't have been a problem and–"

"Just shut up and walk," she said.

The farther they inched into the crevasse, the narrower it became and the higher the walls of ice rose on both sides. Julia didn't like being enclosed. She felt as if the walls were crowding her, as if the air were getting thinner, making her short of breath.

"How much farther?" she asked, her voice barely above a whisper, as if she didn't want the walls of ice to know they were there.

"Beats me," Ben answered. "All I know is that we have to keep going until we find the toboggan. If we go home without it, Mom will know and we'll be dead."

They continued along the crevasse. Under their feet was ice, but also the unmistakable sound of water, dripping from above and probably running below the ice, as well. Julia wondered how thick that ice was and, more important, how deep the water was beneath.

The crevasse seemed to twist like a pretzel, and they could never see very far ahead. Julia stopped glancing up. It just made things worse. She fixed her eyes on her brother's back. As long as he was in front, she was *okay...okay...okay.* With each step she repeated the word, thinking that it couldn't be much farther and soon they'd be able to turn around and–

"There it is!" Ben yelled.

"Keep your voice down!" Julia rasped, reaching forward and smacking her brother on the back of the head.

"Hey, what's the—"

She smacked him again. "Be quiet. You don't want to disturb the ice."

He grinned. "Do you think there's evil spirits in the ice and we might wake them up if I speak too loud?"

"No," she whispered, "but I do think there's such a thing as an avalanche and they get triggered by loud sounds made by jerks."

Ben's smirk froze in place and then faded as he tilted his head and peered at the ice towering over them.

"C'mon, let's get the toboggan and go," Julia said.

Ben nodded and continued on. The toboggan was up ahead, lying on its side. He reached down, turned it over, and examined it. "No damage that I can see."

"Good. Now let's get out of here and—" A look of terror flashed across Julia's face.

"What's wrong?" Ben demanded.

Her mouth moved, but no words came out. She raised a hand and pointed. Ben turned and then saw it. Two legs—human ones—stuck out of the ice...

❄ ❄ ❄

The police chief got up from the desk and strolled out of his office. "I've got to go downstairs and speak to the coroner."

"I hate going down there," his secretary said. "That morgue gives me the creeps every time I walk in."

"Any time I can *walk* in it isn't too bad. I'm more worried about when they'll be *carrying* me in."

"Very funny," she muttered.

He grinned. "I'll be back in a while, so hold my calls."

"I've been holding your calls for two days. There must have been about a hundred of them. I wish those people would just leave me alone and wait until you issue a report."

"They're only trying to do their jobs," the chief said.

"What they're doing is stopping me from doing *my* job," she complained. "I hope you're not expecting those reports on the new bylaws to be finished on time."

"Do the best you can. I'll be back soon."

Carrying a briefcase in one hand, the chief left the office, walked along a short hallway, and entered a stairwell. He descended four flights of stairs until he reached the sub-basement. Fluorescent lights burned overhead, but the corridor was dim and the air heavy. As he moved, the soles of his heavy shoes echoed off the walls. The door at the end of the hall had a sign that said MORGUE. He went in.

"Hello!" he called out in a rich baritone.

"I'm back here!" shouted a voice from behind the door to the autopsy room. "Come on back!"

The chief's stomach suddenly lurched. He didn't mind being in the morgue or around bodies. What he didn't like was seeing bodies being cut up when the coroner was trying to determine the cause of death. The chief certainly wasn't going to tell anybody, but he was pretty squeamish around that sort of stuff.

Under his chin was a faded, crescent-shaped scar, the last trace of an injury he suffered when he was seventeen and in grade twelve. He'd been in biology class and, along with everybody else, was dissecting a cat. At the time he didn't think it would be a problem. He was a big guy. Even at that age he was 1.9 metres and weighed almost 100 kilograms. Not only was he big, but he was tough—a starter on the county-championship-winning football team. And the dissection wasn't a problem...at least until he sank his scalpel into the cat's gut. As a whiff of something bad rose to his nostrils, he fainted dead away, smashing his chin on the counter on the way down. Even now he didn't like to think about the incident.

Slowly, cautiously, he swung his head into the autopsy room. The coroner was wearing a white lab coat and had his back to the door. In front of him was the metal table that held the body.

"Um...I can come back later if you're not finished," the chief offered.

"No, that's okay," the coroner said. "I'm almost done." He turned and began to pull off his latex gloves. The coroner was as little as the chief was big. His grey, thinning hair, flying in a thousand different directions, and the lines that etched his face made him look every day of his seventy-two years. The coroner removed both gloves, balled them up, and tossed them into a garbage can in the corner. "I've got to wash up and then I'll come right out."

The chief felt a surge of relief, nodded, and retreated perhaps a little too rapidly from the autopsy room. As the door closed behind him, he heard running water. He took a seat and the coroner quickly followed, drying his hands on a clean white towel as he emerged.

"So," the coroner said, "how are those kids doing?"

"The kids who found the body?"

"Yeah."

"Better now that they told somebody about it," the chief said. "Can you imagine finding a body and being more worried about what your mother will say about being where you shouldn't be than about report-ing it?"

"I can understand that."

"You can?"

"Sure, if I'd been a kid and went against what my mother told me to do, I wouldn't have said anything because then there would have been two bodies–the one I found and mine. She would've killed me!"

The chief laughed.

"The important thing is that they finally did report it," the coroner added.

"Three days later, and only because the girl was having trouble sleep-ing," the chief said, shaking his head.

"It's pretty disturbing to find a body. Besides, it isn't like three extra days was going to make much difference with this one."

"He's been in that ice a long time, eh?" The chief stroked his chin. "I was pretty shocked to see you on television last night."

"You weren't the only one. I practically spit out a mouthful of coffee when it popped onto the screen."

"Why were you surprised? You knew you'd been interviewed."

"I was interviewed by a lot of people, including that CBC crew. I just didn't expect it to come up as a news flash in the second intermission of *Hockey Night in Canada*, that's all."

"Can you tell me a better place to air a story about an *ice*man than during a hockey game?" the chief asked with a chuckle.

"Very funny. I guess the only thing that surprised me more than the news flash was what a big deal this whole thing has become here in town. Did you know that half the rooms at the hotel are filled with newspaper, television, and radio people?"

The chief nodded. "I saw a couple of those big news trucks parked on the street in front of the hotel. Those are really something with the big satellite dishes and wires and lights and aerials. Pretty darn impressive. And all here because of our iceman."

"Still, how can it be breaking news when the guy's been dead for at least fifty years?"

The chief whistled. "Fifty years? You think he was in the ice that long?"

"That's my guess."

"*Your* guess? I thought you were a man of science."

"It's a hard one to tell for sure. Ice preserves things and stops the usual process of decomposition. I made an educated guess."

"And what exactly did you base that guess on?" the chief asked.

"Mainly the clothing he was wearing."

"Clothing?"

"His clothes are typical of those worn in the early and mid-1950s."

"How do you know that?"

"I'm seventy-two. *I* used to wear clothes like that. I wasn't always this old. Believe me, I was once a pretty stylish cat."

"I believe you, though I wouldn't include that as part of your official report."

The coroner winked. "Want a coffee?"

"Um...I don't know."

"Tim Hortons—only the best down here. Just brewed it up."

"Yeah, that would be good."

The coroner ambled over to a counter, poured out two cups, and handed one to the chief.

"Thanks," the chief said as he took a sip. "Best coffee there is."

"Want some Timbits?" the coroner asked, motioning to the box on the counter beside the coffeepot.

The chief held up his hands. "I'll pass. I don't know how you can eat anything when you're down here."

"If I didn't eat when I was here, I'd have starved to death a long time ago." The coroner reached into the box, pulled out a Timbit, and popped it into his mouth. "I just try to avoid the ones filled with jelly."

The chief shuddered, and his stomach did a somersault. "So what else can you tell me about the body, or do I have to wait until the next hockey game?"

"I can tell you the basics. Male, 1.8 metres, weighed around 79 kilograms, brown hair, brown eyes, left-handed."

The chief raised an eyebrow. "How do you know he was left-handed?"

"He had a watch on his right wrist. People who are left-handed do that."

"And have you determined the cause of death?"

"My best guess is exposure."

"Exposure?"

"He froze to death."

"So you don't suspect foul play?" the chief asked.

"Can't rule that out. He has injuries to his face and a broken leg."

"I saw the facial injuries, but I didn't know about the broken leg," the chief said.

"Left leg, femur. Bad break."

"The femur...that's the big bone above the knee, right?"

The coroner nodded. "It's a hard one to fracture."

"How do you think it happened?"

"I think both the facial injuries and the broken leg are consistent with a fall from a great height—like from the top of the crevasse he was found in."

17

The chief scratched his head. "But you said he died from exposure, right?"

"Yep. The injuries weren't sufficient to cause death…at least directly."

"Can you explain that?"

"Because of the injuries he wasn't able to climb out of the crevasse. He froze over the next few days. Mind you, someone could've pushed him into the crevasse."

"What? Now you're saying he *might* have been murdered?"

"Who's to say? It would really help if we knew who he was. Have you had any luck making an identification yet?"

The chief took another gulp of coffee. "None."

"Not even with the fingerprints I lifted?"

"No match, which just means he was never in jail or in the armed forces."

"How about that notebook that was found with the body?" the coroner asked.

"It was some sort of journal. No names or phone numbers or identification, and unfortunately most of the ink has been blurred and smeared and can't be read."

"But you can read some of it?"

"Yeah, mostly a few lines on each page, but nothing that can help us."

"What about the cameras in the bag you found?" the coroner asked. "Like the clothes, the watch, and a flashlight the man had, they also helped me to establish the age of the body. According to the manufacturers, those models were made before 1960."

"Yeah, the four cameras the guy had in a camera bag were our last best hope," the chief said.

"They're pretty pricey, aren't they?"

"Top of the line," the chief confirmed.

"Were you able to do anything with the serial numbers?"

"Nope. Dead end. But it's not what's *on* the cameras that was helpful, but what was *in* one camera that's important."

"In the camera?"

"The film."

"The film! What good would fifty-year-old film do?"

"It would produce fifty-year-old pictures," the chief said.

"Come on, film in a camera trapped under tonnes of snow for five decades or more couldn't possibly– You developed the pictures, didn't you?"

"We didn't have anything to lose trying." He removed a manila envelope from the briefcase he'd brought down from his office. "Three of the cameras had no film in them."

"And the fourth?"

The chief grinned. "Sixteen pictures."

"That's amazing!"

"It's a pretty special camera that can stay waterproof that long. Here, let me show you." The chief opened the envelope, took out the pictures, and placed them side by side on a table.

"These are beautiful!" the coroner said as he picked up one of the black-and-white photographs.

"They are indeed. This man wasn't just some tourist out taking snapshots on his vacation. He had to be a professional photographer, a well-travelled one, or someone who knew his way around a camera better than most people."

"Had to be," the coroner agreed. "These pictures are from a lot of different places."

"As far as I can tell. Look," he said, pointing at one shot, then another. "This is an ocean, and while I can't put my finger on it, this looks a bit like Newfoundland." He pointed to a third picture. "And this one has a polar bear in it, so it must be somewhere up north."

"And this is somewhere in the mountains," the coroner said, picking up another picture. "Beautiful…any idea where it's from?"

"Not really. Nearest I can figure, these shots are from all over Canada."

"Why would somebody be doing that?"

"Now *that's* a good question."

"I just wish we had an answer," the coroner said. "There must be some reason why… Wait a second. Let me have a look at that notebook."

The chief extracted the notebook from the briefcase and handed it to the coroner. "Be careful. The pages are pretty fragile."

Slowly and with great care, the coroner opened the notebook. At the top of the first page there was the number 1. The first few lines, written in the same ink, were barely legible. Below that the words were blurred and had smeared beyond recognition. He turned the page. The number 2 was atop the page and again just the first sentence could be read. Slowly he continued through the book page by page until he reached the final entry on page 16.

The coroner glanced up and gestured at the pictures. "Didn't you say there were sixteen? That's not a full roll."

"The others were unexposed. And, as you can see, the rest of the journal has no entries. Looks as if our friend didn't get a chance to finish his project."

The coroner rubbed his jaw thoughtfully. "So what do you think? The numbered pages refer to the order of the pictures he took?"

"Something like that. I've marked the backs of these photos with the corresponding numbers, you know, one, two, three, and so on. Do you think there are clues about this guy hidden in the photos or the journal entries or both?"

"Maybe… There's something going on here. Did you notice the numbers in pairs at the bottom of each page of the journal?" The coroner pointed at the first page of the notebook.

"Not really. Hmm, 47 59, 48 35, 47 39…? Seems kind of meaningless to me."

"Maybe not. I think it's some kind of code. Who knows? Perhaps our iceman was a spy!"

The chief frowned. "Now you're really letting your imagination run away with you."

"Let me hold on to the photos and notebook for a while. Ever since I was a kid I've played around with puzzles, ciphers, and secret codes. Maybe I can figure this out. But I think we'll need some help…"

❄ ❄ ❄

A couple of days later the coroner and the police chief stood together on the elementary school gymnasium stage. On the other side of the closed curtain they could hear the muttering, chattering, and laughing of the audience. The chief stuck his head through the curtain and looked at the assembled group.

"Are there a lot of them?" the coroner asked.

The chief closed the curtain. "Full house."

"Then I guess I better get started."

"Just let me introduce you and then I'll go to the back and run the projector. Good luck."

"Thanks."

After the chief made his introductions and welcomed everyone, the coroner slipped between the curtains and strode to the podium. He tapped the microphone with his finger, and sound bounced around the room, silencing the crowd.

"Thank you, members of the media, for coming here to attend this press conference. My apologies for the delay in the originally scheduled time, but we had to prepare a few things first."

Gathered in front of him in the gym were more than fifty members of the media. They sat in four rows of folding metal chairs. On both sides of the chairs there were television crews bristling with cameras and bright lights. Every time the coroner glanced in the direction of the lights he was almost blinded. Two special guests were also on hand–Ben and Julia, the kids who had found the frozen body.

"I'll begin by giving you the information that's been obtained through the autopsy and the preliminary investigation." The coroner quickly gave them the basic facts–Caucasian, male, mid-fifties, brown hair, brown eyes, weight, and height.

"We believe this man fell into the crevasse and suffered facial injuries and a broken leg that made it impossible for him to climb back up. We found a number of cameras with the body and think the man was probably taking photographs prior to his fall. It appears he may have lain at the bottom of the crevasse for some time, resulting in death by exposure due to the cold."

One of the reporters leaned close to a colleague beside him. "I think my headline tomorrow is going to read PHOTOGRAPHER DIES FROM EXPOSURE."

The second man chuckled.

"Are there any specific questions you want answered?" the coroner asked.

"Is there any indication as to how long the man was entombed under the ice?" one of the reporters called out.

"It's difficult to provide an exact date."

"Stephen Bradley, CTV news," a reporter said as he rose to his feet. "Is it possible that he's from prehistoric times—a *true* iceman?"

"Not unless prehistoric man had already invented the wristwatch, the camera, and the flashlight," the coroner answered, and the room burst into laughter.

"Oh...I'm sorry...I didn't know about those things," the reporter muttered as he quickly sat and slumped in his chair, trying to make himself invisible.

One of the newspaper reporters in the back row leaned close to the woman beside him. "Typical television guy. Too busy making sure his hair looks good to bother reading the background notes or listening to the coroner."

"We do believe, however," the coroner continued, "that judging from the unfortunate man's clothing, as well as the cameras, watch, and flashlight we found with him, that he's most likely been dead for about fifty years."

"Have you identified him yet?" another reporter asked.

"Yeah, do we know who he is?" a second reporter added.

"As you're all aware, we didn't find any identification on the body. Subsequently we circulated a picture of the man to the general public, but so far no one has come forward to claim him. Of course, due to decomposition and the man's original facial injuries, his features are somewhat distorted, which would make identification difficult. There was no hit with the fingerprints, and the national missing-persons database indicates no one in that time period who matches the general description of the dead man. So, that brings me to the main reason I've called you all here today. We need your assistance, and the help of the general public, to figure out who this man is and how he came to this end."

Suddenly there was complete silence in the gym as everybody stopped fidgeting and talking and stared up at the coroner.

"Could you please dim the lights?" the coroner asked the police chief. The room darkened, and a beam of light projected a picture of a forest and a ghostly bear onto the screen to the right of the coroner. "This is a picture we developed that was in the only camera belonging to the unknown man that had film in it."

"It's beautiful," a voice called out from the audience.

"Can we use it...can we get copies of it to use in our articles?" a newspaperman asked.

"That's *exactly* what we want you to do," the coroner replied eagerly. "In total there are sixteen different exposures. And we'd like you to publicize all of the pictures. But there's more. The notebook we found with the dead man contained fragments of notes that we believe are linked to the photos."

The screen to the left of the coroner came to life as a beam projected the faded words from the notebook that corresponded to the bear in the forest.

The coroner waited a moment for the audience to digest the words, then said, "You'll also notice the number 1 at the top of the page and some other numbers in pairs–47 59, 48 35, 47 39–at the bottom. Chief, could I have the next slides please?"

Another picture, showing strange rock formations, appeared on one screen, followed by corresponding words on the second screen.

"Now at first we strongly believed there was some kind of code or pattern in the pictures and words that, once deciphered, would tell us who our iceman is, and maybe what happened to him. And although we haven't completely ruled that possibility out, we now think the numbers at the bottom of each page of the notebook might contain the key to our mystery."

As soon as the coroner got the last words out of his mouth, the audience exploded into a babble of voices. The loudest demanded, "Didn't you say this man's death was accidental? If that's the case, what's the big mystery?"

The coroner cleared his throat. "I said he fell into the crevasse, but I didn't say what made him fall."

This comment caused an even greater commotion until a radio reporter managed to be heard. "Are you suggesting he might have been murdered?"

Grinning slyly, the coroner said, "Anything's possible. We know this man was at the bottom of the crevasse for some time before he died of exposure. He had a flashlight and we believe he made these journal entries for a reason."

A reporter wearing a Russian-style fur cap got to his feet. "Jim Anderson, CBC. The next thing you'll be telling us is that this fellow was a spy."

The coroner chuckled. "Like I said, anything's possible. But let me finish, then I'll take more questions or comments. After a lot of digging and consulting with experts, we were able to identify where these pictures were taken. We haven't had enough time yet to check, but we had an idea that the numbers at the bottom of the notebook pages might refer to latitude and/or longitude. Personally, though, I think they're code. And just a few minutes before this press conference I think I might have hit on the key."

The coroner paused either to catch his breath or for effect.

"Well, what are you waiting for?" the CBC man almost yelled. "What is it?"

The coroner inhaled deeply, then continued. "Due to certain repetitions of numbers, I think our iceman has hidden a message in which 35 stands for A, 36 for B, 37 for C, and so on, with Z as 60."

"Why start at 35?" a female Internet reporter asked.

"That's where the latitude and longitude come in again. You see, he might have been trying to confuse people by giving us all kinds of possibilities for patterns or codes—the photos, the words, the numbers. And having 35 to 60 represent A to Z would give him numbers that could be mistaken for real latitudes and longitudes."

"So maybe our iceman was leaving fake clues, like red herrings in a detective novel?" the police chief at the back spoke up.

"Precisely!" the coroner said. "First, however, we have to find out the exact latitudes and longitudes of these photos and see if they match any of the numbers at the bottom of the pages. If they don't, we can rule that out as a code. Then we can see if my number/letter code tells us anything. In any event, we believe that the more people who see these photos, words, and numbers, the better. So we'd like to see them broadcast and printed across North America. By doing so, we hope somebody, or possibly more than one person, will help us solve this mystery."

"Can we help, too?" piped up the simultaneous voices of two children. Every eye in the gym focused in on Ben and Julia.

"Of course," the coroner said. "After all, you two found the body." He smiled at the kids, then returned his attention to the members of the media. "In closing, just let me add that you'll all be provided with a complete copy of the pictures and text. So, let's all pitch in and find out who this man was and what happened to him."

PHOTOGRAPHS

1.

Through the early-morning mist the mighty white
spirit silently appeared. Pausing, silhouetted
against the green of the

47 59 48 35 47 39 43 53 36 49 52 43 53 38 52 35 41 49 56 45 48 49

57 48 35 53

2.

I couldn't but think of a giant—or perhaps a giant's child—sitting, playing with boulders, piling and placing them as if they were merely building blocks.

54 42 39 38 52 35 41 49 48 43 57 35 53 35 48 35 41 39 48 54 49 40

54 42 39 53

3.

Like an exclamation point, defiantly rising above the plains until it scraped the very sky, the whole landscape before me exposed and open. Then I saw them in the distance, at first just specks moving across the flatlands...

49 56 43 39 54 55 48 43 49 48 53 45 41 36 47 59 47 43 53 53 43 49

48 43 48 37

4.

Suddenly it opened up in front of me—a ragged slash of dark, deep, dangerous death standing between me and my destination.... I crept slowly forward.

35 48 35 38 35 57 35 53 54 49 50 49 53 39 35 53 35 37 35 48 35 38

43 35 48 48

5.

The sound of a million voices crying out filled the air with a din so loud I could not even hear myself think! The white against the grey shifted as they took to the

35 54 55 52 39 50 42 49 54 49 41 52 35 50 42 39 52 35 48 38 41 35
54 42 39 52

6.

Coal-black eyes stared back at me, and I
wondered, Did he see me as a curiosity or a meal?
He rose to his great padded feet and

43 48 40 49 52 47 35 54 43 49 48 49 48 39 35 52 46 59 57 35 52 48
43 48 41 52

7.

I listened not with my ears, but with my imagination. There, unmistakably, came the sound of
sword on shield, the war cry of the Viking warrior!

35 38 35 52 53 54 35 54 43 49 48 53 43 45 48 49 57 43 35 47 41 49

43 48 41 54

8.

Hand in hand, the children walked, leading me
not only into the bog, but back into my childhood.
I remembered a time when I could only have been
five years old.

49 38 43 39 54 42 43 53 57 35 53 48 49 35 37 37 43 38 39 48 54 43

57 35 53 50

9.

It was as I'd pictured it those many times I read the story. So vivid, so real that I could almost visualize her—brilliant red hair in pigtails and freckles—disappearing around the corner of the

55 53 42 39 38 43 48 54 49 54 42 43 53 42 49 46 39 36 59 47 59 49
57 48 50 39

10.

I couldn't help but wonder—was it named for the foreboding country or for the men who lived here...the outlaws, bandits, thieves, and bad men who hid in the caves and crevices of the hills?

49 50 46 39 36 39 37 35 55 53 39 43 57 35 53 41 49 43 48 41 54 49
41 43 56 39

11.

For a time it was bigger than Toronto, or Halifax, or even New York—the largest settlement on the continent. Then from the sea and the land came the attack.

47 59 53 39 46 40 55 50 54 49 54 42 39 39 48 39 47 59 43 35 47 48
49 54 35 54

12.

*How could such beauty come from death? The
brilliant reds, oranges, and yellows reflected
against the blue of the water, forming a canvas
painted by the true master.*

*52 35 43 54 49 52 54 42 49 55 41 42 47 59 37 49 48 53 37 43 39 48
37 39 54 39*

13.

The roof was constructed to protect the bridge from the snow and rain, but what would protect the traveller from the spirits that lurked within that covered bridge?

46 46 53 47 39 57 42 35 54 43 42 35 56 39 36 39 39 48 38 49 43 48
41 37 49 55

14.

My feet slipped out from beneath me on the treacherous rocks, and I began sliding toward the edge. I cried out, but my voice was lost in the thunderous roar. Desperately I tried to dig in my heels, and my fingers grasped at the

46 38 46 39 35 38 54 49 35 48 55 37 46 39 35 52 57 35 52 43 42 49
50 39 57 42

15.

The sun dipped into the ocean and its light was extin-
guished. The final whistle blew, signalling the end of
another day of labour. As the machinery fell silent, the
workers abandoned their tasks and retreated to their
homes. There I stood, safe within the shadows. The only
sounds were the wind and the waves, though I could
almost hear the quickening beat of my heart. Should I
leave or enter the now-abandoned building?

49 39 56 39 52 38 39 37 43 50 42 39 52 53 54 42 43 53 47 39 53 53
35 41 39 37

16.

He lowered his head and pawed at the ground. As I braced for his charge, he turned and fled along the path. I hesitated for a second, then followed as he led his harem into the mountains.

35 48 46 39 54 47 59 57 43 40 39 54 35 54 43 35 48 35 45 48 49 57
57 42 59 43 52 39 35 46 46 59 38 43 39 38

FUN WITH LATITUDE AND LONGITUDE

The Earth is an amazingly large place. Maps and globes are just representations, scale models, of the real planet. When you look at most maps or globes, you'll notice there's a grid–a series of imaginary lines that go north and south and east and west. These lines are called latitude and longitude and are used to locate specific spots in the world. Here's how they work.

Latitude lines are horizontal lines that show how far something is north or south of the equator–the very middle of the Earth. The equator is identified as 0 degrees. Going away from the equator, either north or south, each 111 kilometres (69 miles) on average is a degree (each degree increases slightly from the equator to the poles because of the Earth's polar flattening). The very bottom of the Earth–the South Pole– is 90 degrees South, while the North Pole is 90 degrees North. Latitude lines are also called parallels because they never meet.

Toronto, for example, has an approximate latitude of 43 degrees North. This means that Toronto is north of the equator and almost halfway between the equator (0 degrees) and the North Pole (90 degrees North).

Longitude lines, or meridians, are the vertical lines that show how far something is east or west of an imaginary line drawn through Greenwich, England. By international agreement, Greenwich is designated as 0 degrees longitude. The Greenwich line is also known as the prime meridian. The entire world has been divided into 360 degrees of longitude–180 degrees going west and 180 degrees going east. Sometimes the degrees going west are marked with a minus sign (-). Unlike latitude lines, longitude lines do meet at both the North and South Poles where they all come together.

Toronto has an approximate longitude of 79 degrees West. This means that Toronto is west of Greenwich, England, and since 180 degrees is the completely opposite side of the world away from Greenwich, Toronto isn't quite half as far as the other side of the world from Greenwich.

Those are the basics of latitude and longitude. Now let's complicate things a bit. Degrees are usually very far apart. Remember that longitude lines get closer as they leave the prime meridian at Greenwich and actually meet at both poles. To find a very specific place each degree is further divided into minutes and seconds. Between each degree is 60 minutes and each minute is broken down into 60 seconds. It's important to understand that even though they are called minutes and seconds, these divisions have nothing to do with time.

Toronto is Canada's largest city, so it's a pretty big place and the exact latitude and longitude will vary depending on what part of the metropolis you calculate them from. For instance, exact latitude coordinates of, say, 43 degrees, 40 minutes, 12 seconds North, puts you in the vicinity of the central neighbourhoods of St. James Town/Cabbagetown. In short form this is written as 43:40:12 N. This spot would give us an exact longitude of 79 degrees, 22 minutes, 12 seconds West. In short form this is written as 79:22:12 W. With these coordinates anyone can exactly locate this neighbourhood of Toronto on a world map or globe even if no cities or towns are marked. With a global positioning system, or GPS, you could pinpoint your location to the very corner you're standing at or the bed you're lying on in your house.

We want to help the coroner in our story determine the latitude and longitude of each of the places depicted in the photographs found in this book. On page 51 you'll find a chart with the number of each photograph (1 to 16 in the order they appear in this book), a description of each photograph, the exact name of the place, and the province or territory that it's in. The latitude and longitude have been left blank.

DEATH BY EXPOSURE

In order to discover the actual latitude and longitude of each place, go to Natural Resources Canada's "Geographical Names of Canada" Web site at *www.geonames.nrcan.gc.ca.* When you have the site up on your computer screen, click on English or French. On the next Web page go to "Querying Canadian Geographical Names" and click on "Query by Name." When the next page pops up, go to "1. Key in a Canadian Geographical Place Name" and type in a place. For example, the first photograph in this book was taken on Princess Royal Island, so type in that place name. Next scroll down to the list of provinces and tick off the appropriate one. In this case that would be British Columbia. Then click on the "Submit Query" button below the province list. When the next page comes up, click on "Info" under the heading "Details." And there you have it: the latitude and longitude of Princess Royal Island!

To start your next search (after writing down the latitude and longitude of Princess Royal Island), click back to the "Submit Query" page and look for the second place, Mingan Archipelago National Park Reserve. In some instances, you may end up with more than one listing after you submit your query. If that happens, pick the first one in the list.

While you're at Natural Resources Canada's Web site, you might want to see what the latitude and longitude of your own town or city is. That way you'll know exactly where you are in the world. Readers in the United States can check out their latitudes and longitudes at the U.S. Geological Survey's "Geographical Names Information System" Web site at *http://geonames.usgs.gov/gnishome.html.* When the page pops up on your screen, click on "United States and Territories" and follow directions. There's all sorts of interesting stuff to discover on the U.S. Geological Survey's main site (*www.usgs.gov*), too. The same goes for Natural Resources Canada's main site at *www.nrcan.gc.ca.*

Once you've got all the latitudes and longitudes of the sixteen places, locate them by number on the map of Canada on page 50, beginning with Princess Royal Island, which is number 1. You'll notice that the map has a latitude and longitude grid. If you don't want to mark up your book, you might want to photocopy the map and chart.

CANADA

80
75
70
65
60
55
50
45
40

YUKON
TERRITORY
140

NORTHWEST
TERRITORIES

NUNAVUT

NEWFOUNDLAND
AND
LABRADOR

BRITISH
COLUMBIA
130

ALBERTA

MANITOBA

QUEBEC

50

SASKATCHEWAN

ONTARIO

PEI

120

NEW
BRUNSWICK

NOVA
SCOTIA

60

110

100

LEGEND

BOLD= DEGREES OF LONGITUDE
ITALICS= DEGREES OF LATITUDE

70

80

90

50

Photo	Description	Place	Province	Latitude	Longitude
1	Spirit Bear	Princess Royal Island	British Columbia		
2	Rock Formations	Mingan Archipelago National Park Reserve	Quebec		
3	Eagle Butte	Grasslands National Park	Saskatchewan		
4	Crack in Ice	Pond Inlet	Nunavut		
5	Northern Gannets	Bonaventure Island	Quebec		
6	Polar Bear	Cape Churchill	Manitoba		
7	Viking Settlements	L'Anse aux Meadows	Newfoundland and Labrador		
8	Bog Walk Trail	Kouchibouguac National Park	New Brunswick		
9	Anne of Green Gables House	Green Gables	Prince Edward Island		
10	Prairie Valley	Big Muddy Valley	Saskatchewan		
11	French Fort	Louisbourg	Nova Scotia		
12	Lake in Killarney Provincial Park	A. Y. Jackson Lake	Ontario		
13	Covered Bridge	Hartland Covered Bridge	New Brunswick		
14	Waterfalls	Niagara Falls	Ontario		
15	North Pacific Cannery	Port Edward	British Columbia		
16	Deer	Banff	Alberta		

FUN WITH SECRET CODES

People have been using codes, ciphers, signals, and secret languages to conceal messages for centuries. Just who came up with the first secret code is cloaked in mystery, but most historians think the ancient Egyptians are a good possibility. The builders of the Pyramids developed special secret hieroglyphic codes for religious purposes about 4,000 years ago. A little later other ancient civilizations such as the Babylonians, Assyrians, and Chaldeans in Mesopotamia (present-day Iraq) created their own codes to conceal things like valuable formulas for pottery glazes.

Since then all sorts of people, including Buddha, Julius Caesar, Mary, Queen of Scots, England's King Charles I, Benjamin Franklin, France's Queen Marie-Antoinette, American president Thomas Jefferson, and Napoleon, have employed secret writing to disguise everything from battle plans and treason to religion and romance. Spies have probably been around just as long as secret codes, but the Englishman Francis Walsingham, Queen Elizabeth I's spymaster, headed up a legion of agents that's a direct ancestor of the modern era's U.S. Central Intelligence Agency (CIA), Britain's Secret Intelligence Service (SIS or MI6, for whom James Bond supposedly works), the former Soviet Union's Committee for State Security (KGB, now known as the Federal Security Service or FSB and the Foreign Intelligence Service or SVR), and the Canadian Security Intelligence Service (CSIS).

Famous spies have included Benedict Arnold, who betrayed the Yankee colonists to the British during the American Revolution; Mata Hari, the Dutchwoman who worked for the Germans in World War I; and Kim Philby, the British agent who leaked secrets to the KGB in the 1940s and 1950s. In fiction and movies there are all kinds of spies, both serious and comical. Think of James Bond. Or how about Austin Powers and the Spy Kids?

But let's talk about our own mystery in *Death by Exposure*. As the coroner says in the story, the numbers at the bottom of the page in the photograph section may be a secret code that once cracked will reveal a message about who the man in the ice is. So, after you've made sure that those numbers don't have something to do with the latitude and longitude of the places in the photographs, see if the coroner's code key works. Remember, he thinks 35 stands for A, 36 for B, 37 for C, and so on, with Z being 60.

After you've done that and maybe found out who the iceman is and how he got there, you can discover more fun things about secret codes and spies by checking out the Web site *www.thunk.com*. There you'll also find links to CIA for Kids, FBI for Kids, and a James Bond site. Another cool place on the Internet is 42explore (*www.42explore.com*). It has a code page at *www.42explore.com/codes.htm*. If you want to see what the real spies are up to on the Web, make sure you visit the main CIA (*www.odci.gov/cia*) and Federal Bureau of Investigation or FBI (*www.fbi.gov*) home pages. Britain's SIS or MI6 doesn't have a Web site, but its sister organization, the Secret Service or MI5, does at *www.mi5.gov.uk*. As for Canada, take a look at CSIS (*www.csis-scrs.gc.ca*) and the Royal Canadian Mounted Police or RCMP (*www.rcmp-grc.gc.ca*).

PHOTOGRAPHY NOTES
AND WEB SITES

1. PRINCESS ROYAL ISLAND, BRITISH COLUMBIA

Spirit bears, also known as Kermode bears (*Ursus americanus kermodei*), are a rare subspecies of the black bear. One in ten of these animals is born white, and the north coast of British Columbia (particularly on Princess Royal Island) is the only place they can be found. The spirit bear has been in the legends of the Kitasoo and Kitsquatoa people for years and is considered to be a reminder of a time when giant Douglas fir and cedar trees, coastal brown and black bears, wolves, eagles, and wild salmon were plentiful on the coast.

Princess Royal Island, 520 kilometres (323 miles) north of Vancouver and 200 kilometres (124 miles) south of Prince Rupert, is British Columbia's fourth-largest island and is in the heart of the world-famous Great Bear Rainforest. The island has sandy beaches, lowland old-growth rainforest, subalpine areas, and alpine tundra, interlaced with fjords, estuaries, and lakes. In recent times even more intensive logging of Princess Royal has led to growing concern for its future and pressure on provincial and federal governments to turn part or all of the island into a wilderness park.

WEB SITES

Kermode Bears: *www.schoolworld.asn.au/species/kermbear.html*
PBS Online: *www.pbs.org/wnet/nature/ghostbear/html/intro.html*
Spirit Bear Youth Coalition: *www.spiritbearyouth.org*
Valhalla Wilderness Society: *www.savespiritbear.org*

2. MINGAN ARCHIPELAGO
NATIONAL PARK RESERVE, QUEBEC

Twenty thousand years ago, with the gradual cooling of the Earth, ice floes spread over North America, including the Mingan Archipelago. Because of the weight of the ice, the whole continent sank. Later the planet warmed up again and the glaciers began to melt. Two things happened because of that: the elevation in the level of the ocean and the gradual reemergence of the continent. After slowly rising for 2,800 years, the Mingan Islands broke the surface of the water, and nature started to fashion the first monoliths. Created from fragile rock more than 450 million years old, the weird formations are vulnerable to erosion. Sea waves, wind, and seasonal freezing and thawing all contribute to the bizarre sculptures. These limestone giants constitute the largest group of rock monoliths in Canada.

The photograph was difficult to take because the light was very flat and the sky blended with the rocks. In the end, the picture had to be snapped from the nonlit side of the monoliths to create a better silhouetted exposure.

WEB SITES

Canadian Parks: *www.canadianparks.com/quebec/minganp/index.htm*
Parks Canada: *www.pc.gc.ca/pn-np/qc/mauricie/natcul/natcul1-3_e.asp*

3. EAGLE BUTTE, GRASSLANDS NATIONAL PARK, SASKATCHEWAN

Grasslands National Park in southern Saskatchewan represents everything you never knew about the province. The region isn't flat. Instead it's filled with magnificent badland formations, coulees, buttes and, above all else, North America's last remaining grasslands. It's also the place where the last documented buffalo hunt occurred.

You need to watch where you step, though. Rattlesnakes may be hiding in the tall grass. Golden eagles, turkey vultures, peregrine falcons, burrowing owls, coyotes, red foxes, pronghorn antelope, mule deer, and black-tailed prairie dogs are also found in the park.

Some of Canada's colourful western history took place in Grasslands. The most famous incident was in 1876 when Sioux Chief Sitting Bull sought refuge here from the American army after the Battle of the Little Bighorn and the defeat of Colonel George Custer.

WEB SITES

Discovery Channel: *www.exn.ca/nationalparks/park.asp?park=Grasslands*
Great Canadian Parks:
www.greatcanadianparks.com/saskatchewan/grassnp/index.htm
Parks Canada: *www.pc.gc.ca/pn-np/sk/grasslands/edu/edu1_e.asp*
Virtual Saskatchewan: *www.virtualsk.com/current_issue/grasslands.html*

4. POND INLET, NUNAVUT

Nunavut ("Our Land" in Inuktitut) is Canada's newest territory and came into being on April 1, 1999. Originally it was the eastern part of a much larger Northwest Territories. The territory spans 2 million square kilometres (772,000 square miles) and has a population of about 29,000. Eighty-five percent of the people in Nunavut are Inuit, and it is their traditional knowledge, values, and wisdom that shape the government, business, and day-to-day life of the territory. The capital of Nunavut is Iqaluit on Baffin Island.

The Far North can be beautiful one moment under the pink summer sun, and in the next instant it can be terrifying as the ice cracks in a storm and the noise can be heard over a great distance. The photograph was taken at the edge of a crack or lead in the ice between Baffin Island (in the distance) and Bylot Island, near Pond Inlet.

WEB SITES

Baffin Island: *www.baffinisland.ca*
Government of Nunavut: *www.gov.nu.ca/Nunavut*
Nunavut Parks: *www.nunavutparks.com*
Virtual Museum (Inuit History, Art, and Tradition):
www.virtualmuseum.ca/English/Teacher/inuit_history.html

5. BONAVENTURE ISLAND, QUEBEC

Bonaventure Island is just off the Gaspé Peninsula shore in Quebec. The island is home to the world's second-largest northern gannet breeding colony (more than 200,000 birds). Since 1972 Bonaventure has been part of a provincial park that also includes the fabled Percé Rock. The din of the gannets is deafening, the sight unbelievable, and the smell awful.

WEB SITES

Gaspé Peninsula: *www.great-adventures.com/destinations/canada/gaspe.html*
New England Seabirds: *www.neseabirds.com/gaspe.htm*
and *http://membres.lycos.fr/revasse/wildlife.html*

6. CAPE CHURCHILL, MANITOBA

Cape Churchill is near Churchill, Manitoba, on Hudson Bay. The world's largest concentration of polar bears (*Ursus maritimus*) is found here. They come to wait for the water to freeze so they can go out hunting ring seals, their favourite food. Adult polar bears are big. Males can weigh 650 kilograms (1,430 pounds); females 350 kilograms (770 pounds).

WEB SITES

Heritage Canada: *www.heritagecanada.org/eng/news/archived/churchill_e.pdf*
Polar Bears Alive: *www.polarbearsalive.org*
Wildlife Watcher: *http://wildlifewatcher.com/wc/church.phtml*
World Wildlife Fund (Polar Bear Central):
www.wwfcanada.org/en/PolarBearCentral/default.asp

7. L'ANSE AUX MEADOWS, NEWFOUNDLAND AND LABRADOR

L'Anse aux Meadows, home to the only proven Viking settlement in North America, is a UNESCO World Heritage Site. UNESCO is a United Nations organization responsible for promoting collaboration among countries through education, science, culture, and communication. As of mid-2004, there were 754 properties on the World Heritage List (582 cultural, 149 natural, and twenty-three mixed). Eleven World Heritage Sites are in Canada. Besides L'Anse aux Meadows, they include the Haida village of Ninstints on Anthony Island in British Columbia's Queen Charlotte Islands (Haida Gwaii); Head-Smashed-In Buffalo Jump, Alberta; Quebec City; Lunenburg, Nova Scotia; Nahanni National Park, Northwest Territories; Dinosaur Provincial Park, Alberta; Wood Buffalo National Park, Alberta/Northwest Territories; Canada's Rocky Mountain parks; Gros Morne National Park, Newfoundland; and Miguasha Provincial Park, Quebec.

It is believed that just over 1,000 years ago Vikings landed at L'Anse aux Meadows and founded a temporary settlement, centuries before the coming of Christopher Columbus to the New World. As early as 1914, Newfoundlander William Munn suggested L'Anse aux Meadows might be the location of Vinland, one of the names Vikings gave in their sagas to the places they visited in North America. However, excavations didn't begin until after 1960 when the Norwegian explorer and writer Helge Ingstad searched the area. Helge's wife, archaeologist Anne Stine Ingstad, eventually discovered the remains of sod dwellings and workshops. Viking artifacts such as a bronze pin, a spindle whorl, needlework tools, and broken wood objects have also been unearthed at the site.

65

Today, during the summer, a visitor centre features guides dressed as Vikings of the time.

WEB SITES

Canada History:
www.canadahistory.com/sections/eras/Firstcontact/lanxameadows.htm
Parks Canada: *www.pc.gc.ca/lhn-nhs/nl/meadows/index_e.asp*
SchoolNet: *http://collections.ic.gc.ca/vikings*
UNESCO World Heritage Sites: *http://whc.unesco.org*

8. KOUCHIBOUGUAC NATIONAL PARK, NEW BRUNSWICK

New Brunswick's Kouchibouguac National Park is an intricate blend of coastal barrier islands and inland habitats where beaches, sand dunes, salt marshes, bogs, rivers, forests, and fields all come together. There are colonies of grey and harbour seals and sea lions, and in the interior there are black bears, moose, and coyotes. North America's second-largest colony of terns is found here, as well as other birds such as ospreys, bald eagles, and great blue herons.

WEB SITES

Discovery Channel:
www.exn.ca/NationalParks/park.asp?park=Kouchibouguac
Great Canadian Parks:
www.canadianparks.com/nbrunswick/kouchnp/index.htm
Parks Canada: *www.pc.gc.ca/pn-np/nb/kouchibouguac/index_E.asp*

9. GREEN GABLES, PRINCE EDWARD ISLAND

Situated in Prince Edward Island National Park near Cavendish, Green Gables House was built in the mid-1800s. It was originally the home of cousins of the grandfather of Lucy Maud Montgomery, the creator of the spirited, lively, red-haired girl named Anne. The farm inspired the locale for Montgomery's novel *Anne of Green Gables*. The home, grounds, and farm outbuildings depict the Victorian era described in the novel.

WEB SITES

CBC Documentary: *www.tv.cbc.ca/lifeandtimes/bio1996/montgomery.htm*
Green Gables: *www.gov.pe.ca/greengables*
L. M. Montgomery Institute: *www.upei.ca/~lmmi*

10. BIG MUDDY VALLEY, SASKATCHEWAN

The Big Muddy Valley is located in a wide depression of eroded earth and sandstone along Big Muddy Creek in southern Saskatchewan. The badland formations in the valley are the result of flowing meltwater from glaciers that once extended all the way to Lake Superior about 11,000 years ago.

The valley also has a nifty outlaw reputation. It was known as Station No. 1 on the Outlaw Trail that began in southern Saskatchewan and snaked south through Montana, Colorado, and Arizona into Mexico. It's said that Butch Cassidy (the outlaw played by Paul Newman in the movie *Butch Cassidy and the Sundance Kid*) organized the trail and that many other desperados hid there in caves over the years.

The picture was taken from high atop Castle Butte (70 metres/200 feet high), one of the more famous natural landmarks in Saskatchewan.

WEB SITES

BootsnAll.com:
www.bootsnall.com/namericatravelguides/prairie/sep01prairie.shtml
Travel Terrific: *www.travelterrific.com/summer2000/canada_sum00_01.html*
Virtual Saskatchewan (The Badlands):
www.virtualsk.com/current_issue/the_badlands.html
Virtual Saskatchewan (Outlaw Rule):
www.virtualsk.com/current_issue/outlaw_rule.html

11. FORTRESS LOUISBOURG, NOVA SCOTIA

The French founded Louisbourg in what is now Nova Scotia in 1713 after ceding Newfoundland and Acadia (New Brunswick) to the British. Over the next few decades the French turned Louisbourg into a major seaport and continually improved its fortifications. In 1745 Louisbourg was temporarily captured by the British, then returned to the French. However, in 1758 the British conquered the fortress town again. This time Britain demolished most of the fortifications and exiled the town's inhabitants to France. Eventually the new British town of Louisbourg sprang up on the other side of the harbour. In 1928 the ruin of the fortress was declared a National Historic Site, and in 1961 Parks Canada began a major reconstruction. Today Fortress Louisbourg, restored to its 1744-era glory, is a major Canadian tourist attraction.

The photo was snapped near the entrance to the fortress. All of the buildings in the picture are part of this magnificent fortress.

WEB SITES

Fortress Louisbourg: *www.louisbourg.ca/fort*
Louisbourg Institute: *http://fortress.uccb.ns.ca/parks/fort_e.html*

12. A. Y. JACKSON LAKE, KILLARNEY PROVINCIAL PARK, ONTARIO

If you travel the La Cloche Silhouette Trail (named after a Franklin Carmichael painting) in Ontario's spectacular Killarney Provincial Park, you'll come upon a spot that looks out over A. Y. Jackson Lake. Located on Georgian Bay, Killarney, a wilderness park, was one of artist Alexander Young Jackson's great inspirations. Jackson (1882–1974) was one of the famous Group of Seven painters who captured the Canadian landscape with oil on canvas. The other group members were Franklin Carmichael (1890–1945), Lawren Harris (1885–1970), Franz Johnston (1888–1949), Arthur Lismer (1885–1969), J. E. H. MacDonald (1873–1932), and Frederick Varley (1881–1969). The group was founded in 1920.

WEB SITES

A. Y. Jackson Biography: *www.tomthomson.org/groupseven/jackson.html*
Group of Seven Online Gallery:
www.groupofsevenart.com/Jackson/Jackson_intro.html
Killarney Provincial Park: *www.friendsofkillarneypark.ca*

13. HARTLAND COVERED BRIDGE, NEW BRUNSWICK

The 391-metre (1,282-foot) Hartland Covered Bridge in New Brunswick is the world's longest covered bridge. It was originally constructed by the Hartland Bridge Company, which was formed by citizens on both sides of the Saint John River. The wooden bridge was officially opened on July 4, 1901. Two spans of the bridge were swept away by river ice in April 1920. After that disaster, major repairs were made and the structure was covered in 1922. In 1980 the bridge was declared a National Historic Site.

WEB SITES

Hartland Covered Bridge: *www.town.hartland.nb.ca/html/bridge.htm*
New Brunswick Covered Bridges: *http://covered_bridges.tripod.com*

14. NIAGARA FALLS, ONTARIO

One of the wonders of the world, Niagara Falls in the Niagara River is the world's greatest waterfall by volume at 2,832 cubic metres (3,701 cubic yards). Niagara is split in half by Goat Island. The American Falls are 64 metres (210 feet) high and 305 metres (999 feet) wide, with a water flow of 14 million litres (3 million gallons) per minute. The Canadian, or Horseshoe, Falls are 54 metres (177 feet) high and 675 metres (2,214 feet) wide, with a water flow of 155 million litres (34 million gallons) per minute.

The falls were created about 10,000 years ago when retreating glaciers exposed the Niagara Escarpment, redirecting the waters of Lake Erie, which originally drained south, northward into Lake Ontario. Niagara is a magnet for tourists, is a popular honeymoon destination for newlyweds, and has long been a major attraction for daredevils who have vaulted over the falls in barrels, boats, and rubber balls. Perhaps the most famous daredevil was Blondin, who walked over the gorge on a tightrope in 1859.

WEB SITES

History Channel: *www.historychannel.com/exhibits/niagara*
InfoNiagara–History of the Falls: *www.infoniagara.com/d-history.html*
Niagara Parks: *www.niagaraparks.com*

15. NORTH PACIFIC CANNERY VILLAGE, PORT EDWARD, BRITISH COLUMBIA

The oldest standing salmon cannery village on the British Columbia coast is in Port Edward, south of Prince Rupert. North Pacific Cannery, located on Inverness Passage, the northern arm of the Skeena River, was in operation from 1889 to 1958, with a short reprise in 1972 for one more season. Seven hundred First Nations, Chinese, and Japanese workers were employed at North Pacific at the height of its operation. The cannery village was declared a National Historic Site in 1985. Today it's a museum and a reminder of the rural canneries that helped to commercialize the salmon industry and create the racial tolerance that continues to exist in the North. Eighty percent of the old rural canneries are gone forever.

WEB SITE

North Pacific Cannery Village Museum:
www.district.portedward.bc.ca/northpacific

16. BANFF, ALBERTA

Banff National Park, Canada's first national park, is one of the most visited spots in the country. People come from around the globe to see the magnificent Rocky Mountains and get a possible glimpse of wildlife. Banff is part of UNESCO's Rocky Mountain Parks World Heritage Site (see L'Anse aux Meadows for more information about World Heritage Sites).

Blessed with glaciers, numerous lakes and waterfalls, immense forests, and some of the world's most dramatic mountains, Banff also has an abundance of animals, including moose, elk, black and grizzly bears, bighorn sheep, cougars, and wolves. The photo of white-tailed deer was taken outside Banff Springs Hotel. The deer clearly have no fear of people.

WEB SITES

Deer: *www.deerdomain.com*
Discover Banff: *www.discoverbanff.com*
Great Canadian Parks: *www.canadianparks.com/alberta/banffnp/index.htm*
Parks Canada: *www.pc.gc.ca/pn-np/ab/banff/index_e.asp*
UNESCO World Heritage Sites: *http://whc.unesco.org*

NOTE FROM THE PUBLISHER

Go to Beach Holme Publishing's Web site
at *www.beachholme.bc.ca* and follow the home page
link to check your latitudes and longitudes, to find out
more about the secret code in *Death by Exposure,* and
to view the book's photographs in colour.